For Lucky, who was.
—B.J.H.

To my wife, Leah, the woman of my dreams.
—D.S.

THIS IS A BORZOI BOOK
PUBLISHED BY ALFRED A. KNOPF

Published in the United States by Alfred A. Knopf, an imprint of Random House
Children's Books, a division of Random House, Inc., New York.

KNOPF, BORZOI BOOKS, and the colophon are registered trademarks of Random House, Inc.

www.randomhouse.com/kids

Educators and librarians, for a variety of teaching tools, visit us at
www.randomhouse.com/teachers

Library of Congress Cataloging-In-Publication Data
Hicks, Barbara Jean.
The secret life of Walter Kitty / by Barbara Jean Hicks ; Illustrated by Dan Santat. — 1st ed.
   p.   cm.
SUMMARY: Walter, an ordinary house cat, fantasizes about the daring adventures of his alter ego, Fang.
ISBN 978-0-375-83196-6 (trade) — ISBN 978-0-375-93196-3 (lib. bdg.)
[1. Cats—Fiction. 2. Humorous stories.] I. Santat, Dan, III. II. Title.
PZ7.H53153Se 2007
[E]—dc22
2006001280

The illustrations in this book were created in mixed media (ink and acrylic) and Photoshop.
MANUFACTURED IN CHINA
10 9 8 7 6 5 4 3 2 1

First Edition

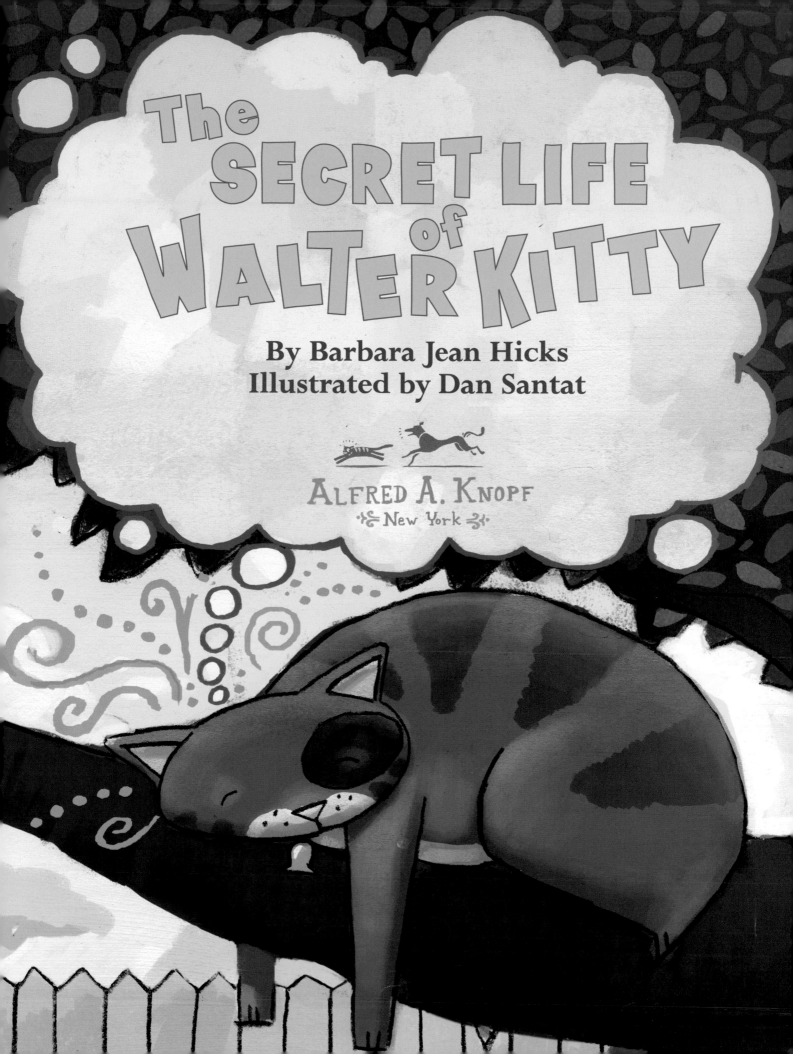

The SECRET LIFE of WALTER KITTY

By Barbara Jean Hicks
Illustrated by Dan Santat

ALFRED A. KNOPF
New York

My Person doesn't know it,
but my real name is Fang.

That's her now. Mrs. Biddle.
If I've told her once, I've told
her a thousand times . . .

Okay, so once in a good long while, I answer to "Wally."

That's Mr. Biddle. He lives
with us. I don't like it,
but for my Person's sake
I put up with him.

I don't know what Mrs. Biddle would do without me. If I didn't help around the house, she'd be

washing dishes

and dusting shelves

and sweeping floors till the cows came home.

Ha. If she doesn't want my help,
I'll help *Mr.* Biddle.

You'd think he'd
be grateful for
my hard work

shaking the rug

and making the bed

and doing the
crossword puzzle.

Does *he* say thank you?

All right, then. If they
don't want my help,
I'll help my*self*.

All that helping wears me out . . .

And Mrs. Biddle wakes me from the most delicious dream.

Okay, so once in a great long while,
I answer to "Kitten."

Catnip puts me in the mood to show
Mr. Biddle a thing or two in the garden.

We plant.

We prune.

We weed . . .

Does Mr. Biddle care?

Nincompoop?
How many times do I have to say it?
MY NAME IS FANG!

I slink inside to tell Mrs. Biddle about it.

Uh-oh. If I don't get busy now with my super-duper-self-clean-scrub-brush tongue, I'm in trouble. *Tub* trouble. Soap. Bubbles. *Water.*

I get busy right away.

After my bath, I feel a nap coming on . . .

And Mr. Biddle shakes me
out of my best dream yet.

Nightmare?

Snookums?!

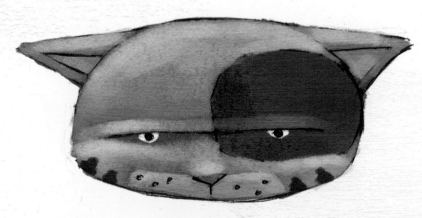

Baby?!!

Then Mrs. Biddle lifts me up and sets
me down on her big, soft lap and finds
the exact spot under my chin that wants
a good, hard skritching. . . .

I confess. Once in a *very* great long while,
I answer to "Baby." But most of the time . . .

Chachi's
COFF
AKERY•MUSIC
Local
Homeless
Restaurant Review
Lickity Split – El Segundo's Premium Dessert Shop
EN

I'm Fang.